UNDER SIEGE

Janice Greene

PAGETURNERS

SCIENCE FICTION

Bugged!
Escape From Earth
Flashback
Murray's Nightmare
Under Siege

SPY

A Deadly Game
An Eye for an Eye
I Spy, e-Spy
Scavenger Hunt
Tuesday Raven

ADVENTURE

A Horse Called Courage
Planet Doom
The Terrible Orchid Sky
Up Rattler Mountain
Who Has Seen the Beast?

MYSTERY

The Hunter
Once Upon a Crime
Whatever Happened to Megan Marie?
When Sleeping Dogs Awaken
Where's Dudley?

Development and Production: Laurel Associates, Inc.
Cover Illustrator: Black Eagle Productions

Three Watson
Irvine, CA 92618-2767

E-Mail: info@sdlback.com
Website: www.sdlback.com

ISBN 1-56254-134-X

Printed in the United States of America
05 04 03 02 9 8 7 6 5 4 3 2 1

CONTENTS

Chapter 1

At 8:32 in the morning, the music on the radio abruptly stopped and a voice came on the air. It was an inhuman voice that sounded like it came from a mouth full of metal. *"Everyone on this island must leave immediately. Those who stay will be put to death. Your largest weapons will be used against you,"* was all the voice said.

Mayor Willard Weston slammed on the brakes. He was a big, solid man with a square face and short red hair. He made a quick U-turn and tore off in the opposite direction, swearing. He was still swearing when he pulled into the parking lot at Cole's Island High School.

The principal was in the office, talking excitedly to another woman. She was saying, "... 'we will use your largest weapons to kill you!'" Both women started laughing, but they stopped when they saw the mayor's face.

"Which class is Brett in this period?" Willard demanded.

"The seniors are in history right now," she said politely. "Room 12. Would you like me to get him for you?"

"Which way is 12?" Willard snapped.

"Just down the hall on the left," she said. Her face looked bewildered.

Willard marched down the hall to Room 12 and flung open the door. The room suddenly went quiet. Willard's angry eyes darted around the room until they fixed on his 17-year-old son.

Brett returned his father's stare, then closed his book and stood up. He was a tall kid, with floppy red hair that he was always shaking away from his eyes. He turned to the other kids. "This is it, folks," he said. "I'm busted. They know about my overdue library book, and they're taking me in. I'm gonna hang at sunrise."

A few kids laughed quietly. Others looked around the room nervously.

Willard wouldn't let Brett talk until they were in the car. "All right. What'd I do?" said Brett.

Willard gave him a disgusted look.

"What'd I *do?* Just tell me so we can get this over with!" Brett cried.

"That stupid prank on the radio!" Willard spat out.

"Dad, I didn't do *anything* on the radio. I swear I didn't."

"If you weren't in the habit of pulling one idiot stunt after another, I might believe you," said Willard.

Brett rolled his eyes and groaned. "So you're carting me off to jail, right?"

"Just be quiet," Willard muttered from between his teeth.

Willard slowed as they reached the town square. In the center was a small park, surrounded by shops and offices.

On one side was the old City Hall. On the other was the radio station, its wide front window catching the morning sun. Several people smiled and waved as they recognized the mayor's car.

"Such a popular guy," Brett muttered sarcastically as he watched his dad's face flush.

Willard pulled into the parking lot next to the radio station. "Come on," Willard said grimly. In stony silence, the two of them walked into the building and up the stairs.

Marjorie, the station manager, was in her office when Willard burst in. Brett was right behind him.

"I want Brett fired right now!" Willard demanded.

"Dad!" Brett howled.

"Willard, please! Slow down for just a minute," Marjorie said in a calm voice. "What's this all about?"

"You know what I'm talking about—that ridiculous announcement!"

"I don't think Brett did that," said Margaret. "Brett takes his job here very seriously."

"I should have seen what a disaster this job would be," said Willard. "It's just too easy for a smart aleck like Brett to make a fool of me when he has the whole island as an audience."

"Could I at least *hear* this thing I supposedly did?" Brett wailed.

Marjorie's face looked troubled. "We don't have anything on tape," she said.

"He did it somehow," said Willard. "No one else here would have pulled a trick like that. Right?"

"Willard, listen . . ." said Margaret.

"Go on, boy, clean out your desk," Willard barked at Brett. "Now!"

"Dad, that's not fair!"

Then a woman's voice yelled from outside the office: *"Marjorie!"*

Stepping out of Marjorie's office, they saw Ilani, the secretary, standing in front of the window. Her face was white.

"Look at that," she cried out.

In the middle of the parking lot, a man and woman were lying face down on the concrete, perfectly still.

A car horn beeped again and again. It was a station wagon, out of control, its radio blaring. They watched in shock as the woman driver frantically tried to turn away from a group of three men crossing the sidewalk.

Seeing the station wagon, the group scattered, but a thin, gray-haired man was too slow. The impact of the crash sent him three feet in the air. The man rolled across the hood and tumbled to the sidewalk. His briefcase flew open; papers scattered over the ground.

The terrified woman leaped from the car and ran to him. Then the car backed up—*but no one was driving it.* The woman screamed and began to run, but the big station wagon was on her in seconds. She screamed again as it hit her. Then she, too, lay still on the sidewalk.

"I'll call the police!" Marjorie gasped. "Ilani, tell the tech room to get out an emergency warning."

"I'll get my cell phone!" said Willard. "We need to call the mainland."

Brett couldn't take his eyes off the parking lot.

A minute later, Ilani returned. "The tech room can't get power. The phone's down—and our computers are, too."

"Tell the technicians to try the emergency generator."

"I already did. They said they can't get power." Ilani started to cry.

Brett saw a woman with a stroller and a small boy heading down the alley toward the parking lot.

"I'm going out there!" he said.

"Brett, no!" Willard shouted. "You're staying right here until we get some kind of plan! I mean it!"

But Brett was already halfway down the stairs.

Chapter 2

Brett opened the back door and looked up and down the alley. Luckily, it was free of traffic.

He sped down the alley after the woman and her kids. It was Jennifer Hartley! She and her husband owned the two gas stations on the island. Jennifer looked up in surprise when Brett ran in front of them.

"Stop!" he gasped.

Jennifer looked confused. *"Brett Weston?"* she cried out in surprise.

Brett heard the sound of a motor starting up. He reached into the stroller and started unbuckling the baby. "What are you doing? Stop it!" Jennifer yelled. She sprang at him, trying to push him away. Sonny, her five-year-old boy, slugged Brett's back with all his strength.

The sound of the motor was very near. "Look!" Brett yelled. A sport utility vehicle had cleared the wooden barrier of the parking lot. Now it was heading toward them, its radio blasting. Jennifer stared at the empty driver's seat, her face going taut with fear.

"Get into the candy store!" Brett yelled. He grabbed the baby and took Sonny's hand.

The SUV's powerful engine roared behind them. They raced inside just as it came to a stop—inches from the store window.

Then it backed up.

"Get behind the counter!" Brett cried.

In a few seconds they were crouching behind the plastic candy bins.

The SUV roared forward. It hit the front of the store with an explosion of shattered glass and splintered wood. The tall glass candy bins in the window crashed to the floor. Thousands of jelly beans, lemon drops, jawbreakers, and maltballs flew through the air and rolled around on the floor.

The huge car backed up again. Now its front end was crumpled and smoke came from under the hood. "No, no . . ." Jennifer whimpered.

The SUV lunged forward. The wall below the window splintered and tore loose. They could see the car's bumper!

Jennifer nodded toward the door at the back of the shop. "Let's get out of here!" she cried.

"City Hall will be safe!" Brett said. "Follow me. Let's cut through the park."

They ran through the doorway just as a terrific crash shook the building.

Now the park was just across the street. Several cars were parked on both sides of the narrow street. Brett saw someone—or something—*red* move between two cars. It was about five feet tall, with limbs as thin as sticks. It looked like a human body without its skin! Brett saw the moving figure for just an instant before it disappeared behind a van.

He turned to the others. Jennifer was grim-faced and sweating. The baby, held tight in her arms, started to cry.

"Ready?" Brett asked.

They took off across the grass. A blue compact was coming after them! "Hurry!" Brett yelled. The car was speeding forward. Classical music played loudly on the radio.

Thinking fast, Jennifer scrambled underneath a concrete picnic table. Brett pushed Sonny in front of him. He felt the car's tire nudge his foot just as it slammed into the side of the table. Sonny screamed and buried his face in his mother's chest.

The car backed off and stopped, its front end crumpled and its bumper dragging on the grass. A loud rattle came from the engine.

On the street in front of the candy

store, a dirty white pickup without a driver backed out of its parking place. Brett recognized it. It was Harold Brayton's pride and joy. The thing was built like a tank.

"Come on!" Brett cried. Jennifer and the kids scrambled out from under the table and ran. But the pickup was speeding toward them.

"Keep going!" Brett shouted.

Sonny was falling behind. Brett pulled him against his chest and kept on going. City Hall was 10 yards away.

Suddenly, the truck roared up behind them. "That tree!" Brett yelled. Now the truck was just a few feet away. Brett grabbed Jennifer's arm and pulled her next to him. The truck hit the front of the tree full force. *Wham!* Brett could feel the heat from the engine. Then it slowly backed away. Only the front bumper was bent. Brett could hear a pet food commercial playing on the radio.

"Climb up!" he yelled. He hoisted

Sonny onto the lowest branch and turned to Jennifer. *"Climb!* I'll hold the baby," he said. Jennifer hesitated. "Go on!" Brett said. "I'll hand her to you."

Again the truck rushed at them! Clutching the baby, Brett dodged behind the tree. *Wham!* The truck rammed the thick tree trunk. Above him, Jennifer moaned. Again the truck backed up. But again, little damage had been done.

Brett tore open the top two buttons of his shirt and tucked the baby inside. He grabbed hold of the lowest branch. As the truck rocketed forward, he swung up onto the branch and held tight, one hand on the baby. *Whack!* The pickup plowed into the tree, making every branch vibrate. Then the engine stopped and started again.

When Brett reached Jennifer, he carefully lifted the baby out of his shirt. Then he saw Sonny. The boy had crawled out onto a skinny branch.

"Sonny! Stop!" he called.

The boy's frightened face turned to him. Then Sonny's feet slipped off the branch. His little body swayed in the air; only his hands held him.

"Mommy!" he screamed.

Brett scrambled onto the branch below Sonny and grabbed his leg. "Let go! I've got you."

"Mommy!"

Wham! With a yell, Sonny fell onto the limb below. Gripping Sonny's leg, Brett slowly pulled him closer, and then gathered him close.

The big white truck backed up again—and stopped. The engine made no sound. The radio was silent. Brett looked at Jennifer. "I think it's out of gas," he said slowly.

"I bet it *is* out of gas," Jennifer said with a tearful laugh. "That Harold's so cheap he never buys more than three dollars at a time."

Chapter 3

"I'll climb up higher and see if there are anymore cars around," Brett said.

He reached the top of the tree and looked out in all directions. Two streets away, he caught sight of an eerie parade. A line of riderless vehicles, one after another, were driving down 6th Street! Even from this distance he could hear their radios blasting.

"See anything?" asked Jennifer.

"Not much. I think we're safe to leave," was all he said.

They climbed down from the tree and walked as quickly as they could to City Hall. Along the way, they listened for the sound of car engines, but the street was empty and silent.

Brett felt guilty. All this time he'd

been trying to help Jennifer Hartley—but what about his dad? Was he okay? Where was he now? Suppose he'd been hurt, or even killed!

Brett's mom had been sick for several months before she'd died. She'd tried to smooth things over between Brett and his father. "You two need each other," was one of the last things the dying woman had said. Brett wondered if his dad needed him now.

The black and gold clock on the front of City Hall said 11:00. Brett led the way up the steps to the tall oak doors, which were cracked open a bit. Sheriff Sam Kettleman was peering out the door. When he saw them coming, he opened the door wide and helped Jennifer with the stroller. The rotunda was crowded with people. Brett saw Marjorie and an engineer he knew from the radio station.

Sam took Jennifer by the arm. "Rick's here," he said softly.

"Daddy's *here*?" Sonny cried.

"Where? Where?" asked Jennifer.

Sam pointed. Jennifer grabbed Brett by the hand and led him over to Rick, who was standing around talking with some of their neighbors.

"Oh, honey, I was worried out of my mind!" Rick cried. Closing his eyes in relief, he gathered up Jennifer and his children in a giant hug.

"Brett saved us," said Jennifer. "He was incredible!"

"You're kidding! I'll never forget this!" said Rick, pumping Brett's hand.

"Sonny was braver than I was," Brett said with an embarrassed grin. "Every time I started crying for my teddy bear he told me I had to hang tough."

Rick and Jennifer laughed. Sam put a hand on Brett's shoulder. "Your dad's over there," he said.

"He's okay?" said Brett.

"Sure. That old guy's too tough to kill," Sam said with a smile.

Willard was sitting at the reception

desk, surrounded by a crowd of people.

"Okay," Willard was saying, "we need any material we can use to block the road—trash, bricks, bags of fertilizer—whatever you can find. And nails, if anyone can find some." Brett stepped up to him.

"Brett!" For a moment Willard looked almost happy to see him. Then his face turned sour again. "Where have you been?" he snapped.

"Just hanging around, wasting time—as usual." Brett snapped right back.

"You're lucky you didn't get yourself killed," said Willard. He turned back to the group he'd been talking to. "Now, has any of you actually *seen* one of these creatures?"

"I have," said Brett.

"Yeah," said Rick. He and his family had just joined the crowd of people around the reception desk.

Willard turned to Rick. "The guy was like skinny and short," Rick said. "His, uh—*skin* looked like raw meat," he added with a disgusted look on his face.

Then the door opened. Three men and a woman carried in an old man. One of his legs hung limply.

"Take him to the Traffic Citations room," Willard called out. "The nurse is in there with the first-aid kit."

"Willard, is someone going for help?" asked a worried voice.

"Three people left for the harbor about an hour ago," Willard said. "They ought to reach the mainland by noon."

A man's shrill voice piped up, "How do you know these aliens haven't taken over the mainland, too? They could be all over the country!"

"They could," said Willard. "We just have to hope they hit Cole's Island first."

Jennifer said, "Willard, Sonny's got an ear infection and I lost his medicine."

"The nurse needs supplies, too," Willard said. "We'd better send someone out to the pharmacy."

"I'll go," Brett volunteered.

"No, I need someone with a head on his shoulders," Willard said curtly. "Anyone want to go to the pharmacy?"

"Brett saved my family!" said Rick.

Willard's mouth dropped open.

"It's *true!*" Jennifer insisted. "Brett ought to get a medal for what he did!"

"I'll go with him," said Rick.

"Rick!" Jennifer cried. Her worried eyes pleaded with him to stay.

"Honey, I can't just sit here and let everyone else risk their necks," Rick said.

"Okay, then—Brett and Rick will go," Willard agreed. "Get the nurse to make you a list."

As Brett turned away, he heard his father whisper to Rick, "Watch out for him." Then Willard called out to the crowd, "All right. Now, we need at least 10 people to set up roadblocks. We'll start by sealing off the square."

A frightened woman's voice called out, "How many people will be run down trying to set up roadblocks?"

"We've got to *try*," said Willard. "Now, who's for roadblocks? Good! I see a hand up! That's the spirit. Who else?"

A few minutes later, Brett and Rick walked down the steps of City Hall. Outside, it was as quiet as a meadow. The only sounds were birds chirping. Brett couldn't see a car anywhere.

They crossed the street and walked down the sidewalk. Grodell's Pharmacy was at the end of the block.

As they approached the barber shop they heard a car engine revving up. Brett got a cold feeling at the back of his neck. He glanced over and saw that Rick looked spooked, too. "We'd better start running!" he cried. They sprinted down the sidewalk.

They heard rock music blaring before they saw anything. Then a sportscar and a minivan came speeding around the corner, their tires squealing.

By then Brett and Rick were in front

of the bookstore. Two wooden carts, piled high with books, stood in front of the big window. Brett looked around frantically. Where could they go?

"Get on the cart!" Rick yelled. The two of them climbed onto a cart just as the minivan slammed into it. The blow jolted the wheeled cart sharply, throwing Rick onto the sidewalk. He was almost buried under a pile of books.

"Watch out!" yelled Brett. He tried to use his weight to turn the cart in the other direction, but it slammed into Rick's arm. Rick yelped in pain.

As the sportscar backed up, Rick managed to scramble onto the second cart. With a hard kick, he pushed away from the wall just as the sportscar sped forward. This time it plowed into the wall, jarring the end of the cart and sending it rolling down the sidewalk.

Rick looked up and saw that the car's hood was now almost twisted off. A moment later, the motor coughed and then stopped running. Brett yelled, "Rick, go back! I'll go on!"

As the minivan roared toward him, Brett stood up on the cart and grabbed the awning. He swung his body up and lifted his legs. The hood of the minivan missed his feet by only a few inches.

Looking down the street, he saw Rick, holding his arm as he ran toward City Hall. Now Brett scrambled onto the awning pole and slowly began to shinny up toward the roof. But his weight was too much. He could hear the screws in the pole bracket pulling loose from the stucco wall. He could also hear another loud shower of shattering glass as the minivan banged into the door.

Just above the pole hung a sturdy wooden sign that said *Island Books*. Brett gently rested a hand, then a knee, on the edge of the sign. In a few seconds he pulled himself up to the roof.

Panting, he stumbled to the middle of the roof and sat down. The overhead sun was hot. His stomach growled, as it always did around noon. He waited. After what seemed like an hour, he saw the minivan drive off.

The buildings in the business district were quite close together. It was easy for Brett to leap from one roof to another. At Grodell's Pharmacy, he lowered himself down to the awning and then dropped to the ground. The street was empty. He opened the door of the pharmacy and walked inside.

The place seemed deserted. Brett walked down the center aisle, trying to remember what was on the list that was still in Rick's pocket.

"Stop right there!" a rough voice barked from somewhere behind him.

Brett turned and stared in disbelief. Oh, no! It was Dave Raybee, a bad-news guy who had dropped out of school last year. Why was he holding a knife?

Chapter 4

Brett rubbed his eyes and took another look. Sure enough, there was Raybee, looking his usual bad-guy self with his shaved head, heavy boots, and torn T-shirt.

Raybee grinned. "Oh, it's you—Mr. Mayor, *Junior*," he snarled.

"I suppose you're here for drugs. Right, Rabies?" Brett snapped.

"Anything I can sell," said Raybee. "Me and my friends got a chance to be the rich kids now. Richer than you."

"Fool! I'm not rich!" said Brett. "But you're always gonna be trash."

"No! *You!*" Raybee lunged at him with the knife. Brett dodged. He grabbed a can of drain cleanser from a shelf and held it ready to throw. Backing up, he kept his eyes on the knife blade. Raybee moved slowly toward him.

"You and your stuck-up friends," snarled Raybee. *"You're* the trash now! Now it's your turn to get kicked around. And spit at! And put down every time you show your face somewhere! Cole's Island is *ours* now. You big sissies are nothing without your cops and your big cars and your stupid cell phones. *We* know how to survive!"

"Put down that knife and I'll show you survival!" said Brett.

The door to the back room slammed. "Stop it, you two! Stop it this instant!" Mr. Grodell marched up to them. He was a small man with a shiny bald spot. But everyone in town knew how sharp he was. His pale blue eyes missed nothing. When he got angry his voice was as hard as iron—and right now he was furious.

"Shame on you. Both of you!" Mr. Grodell said sternly. "The whole island's in danger and here you are fighting each other! Now what's going on?"

"I came for medicine," said Brett. "There's some people at City Hall—"

"What do you need?" Grodell asked.

Brett couldn't remember a thing. "Rick Hartley has the list," he said. "We got separated."

"You just tell me who's there and what's wrong, and I'll figure it out," said Grodell, heading toward the pharmacy counter. He turned to Raybee. "Come on, David. Brett will need your help. And put away that knife until we need to open something."

They filled bags with medicine, bandages, candy, and diapers. "Okay, boys, I've got a scooter behind the building," said Grodell.

"But—" Brett began.

"It's worth trying," said Grodell. "I don't think our visitors found it yet."

Out in the alley, Grodell turned the key and the small engine began to purr with a steady putt-putt-putt sound.

"No radio," Brett said quietly.

"What's that?" said Grodell.

"Nothing," said Brett. He turned to Raybee. "I'm driving."

"Forget that!" Raybee barked. "I've been on way more bikes than you."

"Can you two boys manage this trip without a babysitter?" Grodell asked.

Brett stepped aside and Raybee sat down. Then Brett squeezed himself onto the short seat, the two bags of supplies hanging from his forearms.

"Hurry!" said Grodell. A small green car was coming down the block.

Raybee opened the throttle.

"Get on the sidewalk!" yelled Brett.

They sped down the sidewalk. The car was getting closer, its radio blasting jazz. Raybee stuck close to lightpoles, garbage cans, benches—anything that would shelter them from the car.

They were almost to the end of the street. Just across the way were the broad sidewalk and steps of City Hall. But the green car was almost next to them now. They'd never beat it across!

"Make the car try to hit us!" Brett shouted. "Make it crash!"

"Get off! You're slowing me down!" Raybee yelled back.

Raybee turned around and slowed at the back of a bench. *"Now!"* he yelled. Brett clumsily stumbled off the scooter and fell to the sidewalk.

Raybee let the speeding car almost touch him as he headed for a lightpole. But at the last second, he swerved. Then the car rammed the light pole and the scooter, too. Raybee was thrown to the sidewalk. The scooter landed on its side, its wheels spinning.

Brett ran up to Raybee. "You okay?" he asked. Raybee sat up, rubbing his head. His face and arm were scraped. Blood trickled from his elbow.

"You okay?" Brett repeated. Raybee grunted and stood up slowly.

The car was a crumpled mess. Brett smirked. "Ha! Never crash a cheapo subcompact. It looks even worse than *you* do, Rabies!" he chuckled.

Raybee shot him a look but said nothing. Brett picked up the scooter.

"I'm still driving," said Raybee, reaching in front of Brett to turn the key.

"Be my guest," said Brett.

The engine sputtered for a second and then started up. They drove slowly down the empty sidewalk.

Then, just as they were about to cross the road to City Hall, cars came toward them from both directions.

"Gun it!" Brett yelled into Raybee's ear. "We can beat 'em!"

Raybee glanced back and then swore, his face taut. A police motorcycle was coming after them!

Chapter 5

"Head for City Hall!" Brett cried.

Raybee ignored him. He charged down the sidewalk, driving all the way out of the business district. Then he cut across someone's lawn to the back of the house. Behind that row of houses were fenced-off yards that stopped at the base of a steep hillside.

Raybee drove along the very bottom of the hill, trailing his foot against the slope to keep the scooter upright. The path was too narrow for the police motorcycle. But, through gaps in fences, the boys could see it keeping even with them on the street.

It was rough going. The scooter stalled twice. Once it slid into a fence.

"Watch it!" said Raybee. "Just shut

up and try to keep us from falling."

Brett guessed they were heading for the beach. He knew that the road ended at a small pebbly beach littered with boulders.

As they passed a gap between houses, Brett heard rifle shots and saw the motorcycle swerve. Someone inside one of the houses was shooting at it!

The row of houses ended. Raybee cranked up the scooter for all it was worth and headed toward the rocks. He swore at the scooter to make it go faster. Brett looked back. The motorcycle was gaining on them. In a few seconds it would be on top of them. "It's gonna hit!" he yelled.

Both boys jumped off just as the motorcycle rammed the scooter. When Brett hit the ground, the scooter flew to one side—just missing his head.

Brett and Raybee ran between the boulders. The motorcycle kept coming, first after Brett, then after Raybee. Brett dropped the shopping bags and ran into the water, Raybee after him.

The motorcycle drove a few inches into the water. Then it slowly retreated back toward the road. Brett noticed that a walkie-talkie was strapped to its seat.

The boys waited, shivering in the icy water, until the motorcycle finally backed off and drove out of sight.

"Think it's gone?" Brett said at last.

"Better be," Raybee grunted.

They hurried out of the water and threw themselves down on an open stretch of warm pebbles.

Then Brett looked at Raybee and started to laugh.

"*What*?" said Raybee.

"Your face is blue!" said Brett, his teeth chattering. "What a shame the aliens can't see you now. They'd run off, screaming."

"What did you say, big mouth? You looking for a fight?" Raybee snarled.

"Come on, Dave," Brett laughed. "I'm

just goofing around. I'm not really messing with you, man. I probably look like a wet mop, right?"

Raybee grunted but said nothing.

Brett shook the sand off the shopping bags while Raybee pulled the scooter upright. It wouldn't start. They pulled it to the edge of the sand where the tide wouldn't get it and left it there.

The boys quietly sneaked back behind the row of houses and then in back of the stores. They were passing Giotti's TV store when they heard shouting from inside.

Three guys were in the store. It looked like they were going crazy. The boys could see them rushing from aisle to aisle, taking boxes of equipment off the shelves.

"They're looting!" Brett cried. "We've got to go in and stop them!"

"Oh, let 'em alone," said Raybee. "They're not hurting you."

"What about Stan Giotti?" said Brett.

"The guy's in there working six days a week, trying to make an honest living!"

"I said *forget it!* I know those guys," said Raybee.

The three guys in the store were stuffing portable tape players and mini TVs in their jackets.

Brett was furious. He started walking toward the store. Raybee grabbed his shoulder and swung him around.

"*Don't!*" he said. "I mean it."

Brett was angry. "Take your hands off me! You want to fight about it, Rabies? Yeah? Do you fight as nasty as you look?" Then he and Raybee began to circle each other, their eyes locked.

"I'll *kill* you, little Mr. Mayor," said Raybee. "You don't know nothing about fighting the way I do."

Then the three looters headed out the door and into the street. Each carried a TV or a large sound system. A tall, fat guy held an expensive CD player under one arm. When he got outside the store, he threw back his head and whooped.

Brett heard the radios before he saw what was coming. Then two cars came at them from one direction, and a van from another! Brett saw the panicked look on the thieves' faces. One looter had started to run, zigzagging his way down the street. But the van rammed him from behind. Brett heard a soft thud as the guy's body hit the street.

Then a car swiped the fat guy on the thigh, making him drop the CD player. Within seconds there was a crunching sound as the van backed up over the CD player *and* the guy who had stolen it.

The vehicles turned and drove away, their radios fading to silence.

Chapter 6

Brett's whole body was shaking. He looked at Raybee, and Raybee looked back at him, breathing hard. He was white around the mouth.

Without a word, the two boys started walking. After a while, Brett said, "I don't ever want to see anything like that again. *Ever.*"

"I hear you," said Raybee.

At last they came to the town square. Every street leading into the square had roadblocks made of garbage cans, lumber, furniture, and assorted junk.

As they walked up the wide steps of City Hall, Brett held out the shopping bags to Raybee. "Here, you carry 'em in," he said. "You can be the hero."

Raybee just stared at him.

"Come on!" said Brett.

Raybee gave him a long look as he took the bags. "They're still not going to want me in there," he said softly.

But this was Raybee's day to be Santa Claus. People crowded around him while he handed out diapers and baby formula, candy bars and medicine. The nurse gave him a hug. He had brought her painkillers and bandages.

Before now, Raybee had only come to City Hall to pay a speeding ticket or spend a night in a jail cell. But if anybody in the crowd knew that, they didn't mention it.

Sonny ran up to Brett. "You know when the aliens said they'd use our biggest weapons?" he said. "Is that because they don't know about planes and tanks and aircraft carriers?"

"I guess," said Brett. "Maybe the first thing they saw here was a car accident. Maybe that's why they figured cars were our worst weapons."

"Well, cars aren't *war* weapons—but they can kill people," said Sonny.

Brett smiled, gave the boy a hug, and wandered over to the crowd around his dad. There were more people here now than there were this morning. Raybee had emptied the shopping bags and was hanging around at the edge of the group, not sure if he was welcome.

Brett took Raybee's shoulder and led him up to the front. "Hey, what's up, Pops?" he said cheerfully.

Willard frowned at his son and then looked sharply at Raybee—as if trying to remember who he was. Then he said, "The Valdez brothers are on their way to the mainland. A group went down to the harbor with them. Herm McCollough took his hunting rifle."

Brett nodded. The Valdez boat, the *Rosalita,* was the fastest on the island.

"We've also sent out people to set up more roadblocks," Willard added, "and a search party went off to the clinic to see if anyone's around. We need another nurse or doctor here."

Brett said, "Dad, I've figured out something. It seems the aliens can control anything that has a *signal.* They controlled the radio station when they made that announcement. They shut down the phones and computers. And when the unmanned cars are on the move, their radios are always on. But we rode a scooter *without* a radio—and it worked normally."

"Hmmph!" Willard grunted. "Maybe. But that's useless information at this point. We should be getting help from the mainland soon."

Brett turned to Raybee. "I am so dumb!" he said. "I should have had *someone else* tell him how the aliens operate—anybody but me! Then he would have taken it seriously."

"That will be enough, Brett," Willard growled.

"Don't worry," Brett said to Raybee,

who was looking even more nervous and uncomfortable. "He won't yell at me in front of everybody. After all, the mayor must keep his dignity."

Then the doors opened wide and several people came in. A hush fell over the crowd. Herm McCollough led the way. In one arm he was holding his hunting rifle. His other arm was around Bobby Valdez's 12-year-old son, Diego. The boy's face was streaked with tears.

"They're *dead!*" Diego said in a shaky voice. He hid his face in his hands and sobbed. A woman in the group put her arm around the boy and led him from the room.

Herm McCollough told the story. "We had a tough time getting over there. At 4th and Seadrift, about six cars came after us. We ran like rabbits. Ginny Warren got hit, but not too bad. Just broke her ankle. We left her with a family on 4th. All these people were watching from their houses. One of them ran out and pulled poor Ginny in.

"The rest of us hid in those pipes they laid out for the new sewer project. We waited in those pipes for quite a while. Then, finally, the cars all drove off."

Lena Poblete put her arm around Herm. "He killed one of them," she said.

Herm smiled grimly. "Looks like I did. I shot one of 'em and it didn't get up. So I guess you *can* kill 'em."

He went on, "We made it to the harbor, and Bobby and Len got in the *Rosalita.* But when they started her up, she just went out of control. Bobby was at the tiller, then both of them were pulling at it, trying to make it work. But it didn't make any difference. She just went crazy, going in circles and banging into other boats. Then she got going full speed and rammed the end of the dock."

Herm's voice went hoarse. "The gas tank blew. We must have been 20 feet away, but we could feel the heat of it. And it was loud enough to bust your eardrums. We thought the noise would bring on the cars again, but they stayed away. It was as if they *knew* the boat was going to wipe us out."

There was a long silence. Then, finally, Willard said, "You've seen a lot of what these aliens can do, Herm. Any ideas for our next step?"

Herm said slowly, "When I shot that one, I thought maybe we could put up a good fight with guns. But so far, they're a lot better at killing us than we are at killing them."

"They must have got to the boat's *loran*. You know—its radio navigation system," said Lena. "They must be using it to control the boat just the way they control the cars."

"Couldn't we just let the cars run out of gas?" someone suggested. "It's bound to happen eventually."

Another voice rang out. "And be stuck in our homes like rats in a cage until then? I say, *fight 'em!*"

"Right! Let's go after 'em!" one of the men yelled in agreement.

Everyone started talking at once. Brett turned to Lena and said, "I've got an idea. What if they can only control signals right here on the island? Let's get a Citizens' Band radio. If we put the CB in a motorboat and take it five miles out, maybe we can call for help."

"Now, that's an idea that just might work," said Lena. "Willard!" she shouted, "We've got a plan here!"

Willard called for quiet. Lena looked at Brett. "*You* tell him," Brett insisted.

Lena repeated Brett's idea. Willard thought a moment. Then he said, "I guess that's worth a try. Anyone here have a motorboat?"

"I do," said Marjorie. "But the key's in my desk at the radio station."

"Okay, we'll go there first," said Willard. "Who wants to go?"

"I'll go." It was Sheriff Kettleman.

Willard frowned. "Sam, *I'm* going—

so I need you here. I'll take Ernie."

"I'm going!" cried Lena. "There's a CB in my boat, too."

"Great," said Willard. "Herm? We could sure use your rifle."

"Count me in," said Herm.

"Raybee and I are going," said Brett.

Willard shook his head.

"It's *my* idea," Brett said stubbornly.

Lena nodded. For the second time that day, Willard looked at his son in a new light—almost with respect.

Greg Simms and Deputy Ernie Navarro also stepped forward. "That's enough," said Willard. "Let's get going."

They stepped out the door into the silence of the empty street. Just then the clock overhead struck four slow, solemn notes. In his 17 years on Cole's Island, how many times had Brett heard that clock strike? Five hundred? A thousand? But this time, the sound made the hair on the back of his neck prickle.

Brett looked out over the town square. The roadblocks were still in place. With Willard in the lead, the little group quickly walked around the piled-up garbage cans, furniture, and trash that blocked the street and most of the sidewalk. Nobody said a word. They were all listening.

They had reached the park lawn when Ernie yelled, "I hear them!" Everybody started to run.

Across the park, they could see cars revving up behind the roadblocks. Lena, who was running next to Brett, grabbed his shoulder. "Look!" she yelled, pointing behind her.

Just beyond the piled-up junk was a schoolbus, its motor roaring as it pushed up against a sofa piled with junk. At the other corner, Brett saw the open top of a jeep.

They all ran faster. Greg tripped and fell, but he got up immediately, his nose bloody. Now they were more than halfway through the park.

At the other end of the park, an SUV was shoving two garbage cans aside. A second SUV was slowly climbing over some piled-up bags of concrete mix. The schoolbus and the jeep had almost made it through the barriers!

Brett's breath burned in his chest. He kept his eyes on the big window of the radio station. Every step brought him closer, closer. . . .

"They're *coming!*" Willard yelled.

A swarm of cars came toward them from four directions. The little group scattered. Herm scrambled up a tree. Ernie ducked under a picnic table, his gun drawn, along with Willard and Raybee. Greg and Brett ran behind trees.

Lena dodged behind a tree just as the schoolbus came at her. The SUVs began banging the picnic table as Ernie aimed and fired at their tires.

The jeep, a broken window frame hanging from its bumper, was coming after Brett. "Over here!" Herm yelled from a nearby tree. Brett sprinted forward, grabbing a sturdy branch and swinging his legs up.

Wham! Just as the jeep hit the tree, Herm dropped from his treetop perch into the empty passenger's seat. He immediately began to pound the radio with the butt of his rifle.

The jeep roared backward about 20 feet, then charged the tree again. Herm ducked, just in time. *Wham!* The jeep backed up again and headed for the bench. Brett saw Ernie take aim at the tires just before it hit. *Thud!* A corner of the concrete picnic table broke off and fell to the grass.

One of the jeep's tires spun against

the picnic table bench, as if it were trying to climb it. Slowly but surely, the vehicle inched up, higher and higher.

"It's gonna flip!" screamed Brett. "Get out, Herm!"

He saw Herm begin to scramble out of the jeep, his face deathly white. Then it went over. One of Herm's legs was trapped underneath!

"Get me out of here!" yelled Herm. Raybee started to crawl out from under the table, but Greg got to Herm first. He began pulling on the man's arms.

"Greg! Behind you!" yelled Lena.

As Greg turned he saw that the schoolbus was almost on top of him. *"Run!"* screamed Brett. Greg held up his hands, his mouth frozen open. Then the schoolbus made contact, and the jeep crashed to the ground. Brett closed his eyes and winced.

Now only one vehicle was moving. One of the SUVs was slowly backing away. The rest stayed where they were, their radios silent and their motors off.

When the SUV was out of sight, Willard led the others to the wreck of the schoolbus and the jeep. "They were good men, Greg and Herm," Willard said quietly. The others nodded. Lena wiped a tear from her cheek.

"We better get going," Ernie said.

Lena was looking at the other SUV. "Why isn't this one moving?" she asked. "It's not wrecked."

"Why don't *we* use it?" said Brett. "It looks like it's not in their control anymore."

Brett started to climb up to the seat, but Ernie put a hand on his shoulder. "Hold on, son," he said. "We need to destroy the radio first. Look around and we'll find a brick or something."

"Okay," said Brett.

"Let's go to the radio station now. We can come back here later," said Lena. "Let the aliens think we've disappeared for a while."

They hurried across the park to the radio station. Ernie said, "You folks get inside and stay near the door. I'm going to have a quick look around." He drew his gun and went quietly up the steps.

They waited. Brett noticed his dad looking sharply at Raybee.

A few minutes later, Ernie's voice called down the stairs, "Okay, come on up. The place is deserted."

It seemed strange to be walking through the silent station. Brett had never been there when the radio wasn't broadcasting one program or another.

A cold cup of coffee and a half-eaten donut lay on Marjorie's desk. Just as she had said, the key to her motorboat was in the top desk drawer.

Ernie stepped out of an office carrying a heavy paperweight. "Looks like we're all set," he said. "Let's go."

Willard gave Raybee a hard look and said sternly, "*He's* not coming with us. I just remembered who he is."

Chapter 8

"Dave Raybee's a punk and a thief," Willard snapped. "I don't want him to be part of this group." He turned to glare at Raybee. "As soon as we can possibly manage it, I'm taking you back to City Hall. Sam can keep an eye on you there," he said.

Raybee said nothing, but his head was hanging down, and the back of his neck had turned red with shame.

"But Dad, he's *helping* us!" Brett cried. "Why can't you give somebody a chance once in a while?"

"Forget that. Let's get going before any cars come back," Ernie said.

Nobody argued with that.

A few minutes later, Ernie smashed the radio to pieces with the heavy paperweight. Then he climbed into the driver's seat. Brett felt his heart pounding as Ernie turned the ignition key. The engine roared to life.

Raybee glanced around nervously. "Nothing yet," he said.

This is too easy, Brett thought.

Everyone got in. "Who wants to drive?" Ernie asked. "I need to sit near an open window. You know—in case I have to use my revolver."

"Raybee's good," said Brett. "When we got the medicine—"

Willard interrupted. *"I'll* drive," he said with a frown.

They headed slowly down 4th Street. With the tires flopping uselessly on the rims, the SUV could only move at a crawl. The snail-like pace put Brett's teeth on edge. As they passed by a row of houses, he saw curtains being pulled aside a few inches. Frightened faces stared out at them. "They're like mice in their holes," he thought. "They're wondering where the cats are right now."

"Look," Raybee muttered, tilting his head. Off to the left, a line of driverless cars headed slowly toward 4th Street. The parade of cars cast long shadows in the late afternoon sun.

"They're behind us, too!" Lena cried in a tight voice. "And look over there."

In all, *three* lines of cars were headed toward 4th Street.

Up ahead, they saw two lines merge into one. And just behind the crawling SUV, the third line was getting closer.

"I think we should join them," said Willard. "We can't outrun them—and I'm afraid they'll batter us to bits if we try to escape."

Nobody had a better idea.

In a few moments, their SUV was boxed in by a car behind and a car in front. Music and chatter from the blaring radios filled the air. Although the line moved slowly, Willard had to push the gas pedal almost to the floor in an effort to keep up. Beads of sweat rolled down his cheeks.

They had just entered the poorer part of town. Yards here were much smaller and houses needed paint. Up ahead, Brett could see the smokestack of the island's only factory.

The line of cars turned toward the factory parking lot. As the SUV rounded the corner, Brett looked into the lot. What he saw there almost washed him away in a wave of fear.

The parking lot was full. But instead of being lined up in neat rows, the cars formed a snake-like line. And aliens were moving around between the cars—dozens of them!

"Everyone get down!" Willard cried in a hoarse whisper. He sunk as low as he could in the driver's seat.

The cars in front of them eased into place and stopped moving. Bitter fumes of exhaust filled the air.

Brett crouched below the window

and peered out. The aliens were holding round, black objects the size of golf balls. They were pointing these objects at the cars. Brett guessed they had to be some kind of remote controls. One alien walked close to the SUV. Brett stared with horror at its spindly limbs, raw-looking skin, and small, glassy eyes.

Then suddenly the alien thrust the remote device back and forth. In the next instant a high-pitched whirring sound filled the air. Brett couldn't tell if it came from the remote control or the alien. Then more whirring sounds came from all directions. All the aliens started heading toward the SUV, their red heads jerking forward. The volume of the whirring quickly became a deafening scream.

"They're onto us!" yelled Brett. "Let's get out of here!"

Chapter 9

With Willard in the lead, the group burst out of the SUV into a sea of red bodies. Brett shrank back as the wet red skin brushed against his arms. Ernie fired left and right. Some aliens fell, but the others scattered, waving their remote controls in the air.

Engines roared to life. All over the lot cars began backing and turning. The sounds of engines and gunfire, along with the awful whirring and the blasting radios, made Brett's head ring. He and the others ran out of the parking lot and toward the houses.

"Over here! Over here!" People were waving and calling from the front of one house. Its yard was barricaded by concrete blocks.

The group started running, with five cars speeding after them. "Hurry! *Hurry!* They're coming!" Men and women from the house jumped over the concrete blocks and ran out to meet them. A woman with wild gray hair was armed with a hunting rifle.

They had almost reached the house when Ernie screamed. "They're hit!" someone cried out. Brett turned to see Lena and Ernie on the ground. A station wagon next to them began to back up, getting ready to strike again. Then one man hurled a concrete block at its bumper, and the big station wagon came to a grinding halt.

Then a tall girl called out, "Dave! Dave!" as she threw bricks in front of the other cars. Four men lifted Lena and Ernie and carried them to the barricade.

They all hurried into the house. The woman with the hunting rifle got off a few shots at the station wagon's tires, and then slammed the door.

Two of the cars shoved weakly against the barrier before giving up. There was no sound from the cars' radios. Gradually, they stopped moving, sinking lower and lower as their tires went flat. Sensing defeat, the other three cars on the street slowly backed away.

Inside the house there must have been 25 people. Ernie and Lena were gently laid down on the living room floor. Everyone gathered around. Lena's leg was injured. Ernie said that his body hurt all over. His face was badly scraped from landing on the street.

The gray-haired woman gave out orders: "Somebody get some aspirin. And we need some rolled-up newspapers and tape so we can splint that leg. And blankets." She turned to Willard, "Now what on earth were you doing in the parking lot? Did they catch you or something?"

"In a way," said Willard.

"We're trying to get to the harbor,"

Brett explained. "Our plan is to take a boat out about five miles—beyond where the aliens can control the signals. From there we're going to call the mainland for help."

"Hey, buddy, aren't you the mayor?" one of the men asked Willard.

"Yes. I am," said Willard.

"Imagine that! We sure don't see much of you around this neighborhood, Mr. Mayor," the gray-haired woman said sarcastically.

Willard faced her. "You're right," he said, "but you folks risked your lives for us, and I'm truly grateful for that. Will you help us get to the harbor?"

"Sure," she said. "And maybe you can pay us a visit around election time—if there's any town left, that is. Now, what do you need?"

Willard hesitated.

"How about some bikes?" Raybee suggested. "We could take them down the narrow dirt alley."

"That path goes all the way to the harbor?" Willard asked.

"Sure. Straight to it," said Raybee.

The orders were quickly given. Several men and women went out the back door, covered by the hunting rifle.

"You guys want some popcorn?" someone called from the kitchen.

A big metal bowl of popcorn was put on a table. It was barely warm—but to Brett it tasted like the best thing he had ever eaten. They sat at the table on rickety metal chairs. The tall girl came up behind Raybee and put her arms around him. She had a pretty face and dark brown hair that looked soft as silk.

Raybee looked pleased. "Where were you, Shauna?" he asked.

"Right here, with the rest of the neighborhood," she said. "I've been sick wondering where *you* were."

"Your sister was worried sick about you," someone said.

"I took care of him," said Brett.

The girl looked at Brett with wide gray eyes and smiled a little. Suddenly, Brett wanted to know her better.

The back door opened. "We've got 'em—three bikes," a man's voice called out. Brett quickly took a last mouthful of popcorn. Raybee walked over to Ernie and drew his gun from its holster.

"Hey!" Willard jumped up and grabbed Raybee's wrist.

"Come on, man! I've been shooting beer cans since I was 10," said Raybee.

Willard hesitated, but still kept a tight grip on Raybee's wrist.

"Can't I fight for my town the same as you?" Raybee demanded.

Willard looked around. Every eye was on him, waiting for an answer. "Oh, all right," he said. "Let's go."

Outside the back door was a narrow alley of hard-packed dirt. The bikers had to ride around ruts and bumps and abandoned toys. Brett couldn't remember ever seeing his dad riding a bike.

Willard wobbled behind them, puffing.

Looking down the narrow alley, Brett could see the long wooden docks just ahead. Several boats were tied up on either side. He put down his head and pedaled faster.

At last they came to the end of the alley: Raybee first and then Brett, with Willard chugging along behind. The sun was low on the water, turning the tips of the waves to gold. Raybee had almost reached the dock.

Then suddenly a police motorcycle darted out from behind a house and came roaring after them.

"Dad!" Brett screamed. Willard pedaled madly for the dock. But the speeding motorcycle, its engine howling, rammed into the back of his bike. The bike shot into the air, and Willard was flung 20 feet forward. He rolled over twice—and then lay still.

Chapter 10

"Dad! *Dad!*" Brett jumped off his bike and ran to him. The motorcycle backed up, then charged again. Raybee picked up Willard's twisted bike and threw it at the motorcycle. The impact crashed the motorcycle to the ground in a tangle of metal and rubber. Finally it lay on its side with its wheels spinning and blue smoke coming from the exhaust.

Willard tried to get up. He was bleeding from a cut on his head.

"Let's get him into the nearest house," said Raybee.

"No!" Brett cried. "We're taking him to the mainland."

They half-led, half-carried Willard along the dock. The older man was wobbly on his feet. While Raybee went to get Lena's CB and a flashlight, Brett gently lowered his father's trembling body into Marjorie's motorboat. Then he took off his shirt and carefully wiped the blood from his father's head.

It was hard to move in the boat with Willard stretched out in the middle of it. But Raybee took the tiller while Brett sat with his father's head between his feet.

They chugged out of the harbor into the setting sun. When Cole's Island was out of sight, Brett turned on the CB. But immediately, the boat started to thrash, so he switched it off. "Lucky there's nothing here to hit," he said.

When the sun set, they tried the CB again. This time the boat stayed calm. Brett hesitated. "How am I going to explain all this to the radio operator on the mainland?" Brett asked. "No one's ever going to believe me!"

"So *lie*," said Raybee.

Brett grinned. He turned the CB to Channel 9, the emergency channel, and held the microphone to his mouth. "Emergency situation on Cole's Island," he said. "A violent cult has taken over the entire town. Bring help. Come by boat. And be sure to turn off your *loran* as you begin to approach the island." He repeated the same message over and over. As it grew dark, they could finally see the tiny lights of the mainland across the water.

Beneath his son's feet, Willard stirred. "I can't find my shoes," he muttered.

Raybee looked worried. "Do you think there's something wrong with his brain?" he asked.

"Yeah, I think he's got a concussion," said Brett. "A guy on the football team sounded just like that when he got hit in the head. I just hope it's not too serious."

"You're lucky, having him for an old man," Raybee said. "Everyone in town looks up to him."

"We don't get along so well," said Brett. "He's always yelling at me."

"That's 'cause you've got a mouth," said Raybee. "My old man would pound me flat if I talked the way you do."

Brett thought about that. "Yeah, I guess I do needle him a lot," he said. "But he drives me crazy. 'Don't do this!' 'Cut that out!' 'You're grounded!' Heck, I'm grounded about every other week."

"My old man doesn't care *what* I do," said Raybee.

"Lucky—" Brett muttered.

"Nah. You don't get it, man. He doesn't care if I go or stay. Live or die," said Raybee.

Brett felt embarrassed. Compared to what Raybee was dealing with, his complaints sounded babyish.

The motor chugged along evenly, drawing them nearer and nearer to the lights of the mainland. Brett kept thinking about his dad—and about the tall girl he'd met that day.

"Is your sister going out with anybody?" he asked.

"What's it to you? Don't get any ideas," Raybee growled.

"Hey, I'm not so bad," said Brett. "She seems really nice—except she's got this psycho brother."

"Psycho, yeah. So watch out. And Shauna's got a mouth on her, too, so she'll . . . what's that?"

Brett laid a hand on Raybee's arm. "Listen!"

A boat was coming—no, several boats! Brett waved his flashlight. An answering beam of light immediately shone on them. A long white boat drew near.

"It's the Coast Guard!" Raybee cried.

Brett and Raybee slapped hands.

Then Brett leaned down and said quietly, "The Coast Guard's here, Dad. Cole's Island is gonna be all right—and you are, too." Willard reached out, as if searching for something. Brett took his father's hand and held it tight.

Epilogue

The encounter between the Coast Guard and the alien invaders was brief. An early-morning battle in the factory parking lot resulted in the deaths of three Coast Guardsmen and 17 aliens. The alien bodies were later shipped to several universities for study.

The surviving aliens retreated to the woods, surrounding the trailheads with vehicles. Coast Guard forces waited several hours before they were sure that the vehicles were no longer attacking them.

A small group entered the woods. No aliens were found, but tracks made by the invaders led to a large clearing. The Coast Guard decided that some sort of spacecraft must have carried them away—although neither any members of the force nor the people of Cole's Island had seen such a craft.

Several months later, scientists at Palomar Observatory in California concluded that the aliens had come to Earth from a dying star in the Constellation Cepheus.

Willard Weston was diagnosed with a minor concussion. His doctor ordered him to spend two days in bed and stay away from the office for a full week. Brett made sure his father followed the doctor's orders completely, even though Willard insisted he was ready to return to work after two days.

As soon as his dad recovered, Brett called Shauna Raybee. He asked her to go out with him to see a movie—and she said yes.

COMPREHENSION QUESTIONS

RECALL

1. What did the mysterious radio announcement order Cole's Islanders to do?
2. Why was Willard Weston so distrustful of Dave Raybee?
3. What insulting nickname did Brett use for Dave Raybee?

DRAWING CONCLUSIONS

1. What were the aliens using to control the driverless vehicles?
2. Why did Brett think the aliens might have used cars as weapons?
3. What did Brett have that Raybee envied?

WHO AND WHERE?

1. When Willard Weston heard the mysterious radio announcement, who did he blame?
2. Where did Willard set up Cole's Island's emergency headquarters?
3. Who came up with the idea to take a CB radio out to sea to contact the mainland?

ANALYZING CHARACTERS

1. What two words could describe Mayor Willard Weston? Explain your thinking.
   •*impatient* •*sentimental* •*respected*
2. What two words could describe Brett Weston? Explain your thinking.
   •*indifferent* •*clever* •*sarcastic*
3. What two words could describe Dave Raybee? Explain your thinking.
   •*tough* •*privileged* •*surly*

BEFORE OR AFTER?

1. Did Dave Raybee see his sister *before* or *after* he told Brett to leave the looters alone?
2. Did Brett see an alien *before* or *after* Willard did?
3. Did Rick's arm get hurt *before* or *after* Brett climed up on the roof of the book store?
4. Was Willard thrown off his bike *before* or *after* Herm McCollough was killed?